W9-BYE-748

SIX EMPTY
POCKETS

written by
Matt Curtis

illustrated by
**Mary Newell
DePalma**

Children's Press®
A Division of Scholastic Inc.
New York Toronto London Auckland Sydney
Mexico City New Delhi Hong Kong
Danbury, Connecticut

For my young friend,
Charles Crittenden – M.N.D.

Reading Consultant
LINDA CORNWELL
Learning Resource Consultant
Indiana Department
of Education

Library of Congress Cataloging-in-Publication Data
Curtis, Matt.
Six empty pockets / by Matt Curtis ; illustrated by Mary Newell DePalma.
p. cm. — (Rookie reader)
Summary: Charles's six empty pockets come in handy for carrying such treasures as
a blue star marble, an old crow's feather, and seven striped stones.
ISBN 0-516-20399-1 (lib. bdg.)—ISBN 0-516-26253-X (pbk.)
[1. Pockets—Fiction.] I. DePalma, Mary Newell, ill. II. Title. III. Series.
PZ7.C9445Si 1997
[E] —dc21
96-49441
CIP
AC

Charles's favorite pants
have six empty pockets!

Charles drops a blue star marble in his right front pocket.

In his left back pocket,

he packs a
tractor-trailer truck.

In his two side pockets,
his mother slips a sandwich . . .

. . . and a sweet, golden pear.

He pokes an old crow's feather,
black and shiny in the sun,

in his left front pocket.

And for good luck,

in his right back pocket,

he stashes seven
striped stones.

After lunch . . .

. . . he stuffs his side
pockets full of seedpods
from a honey locust tree.

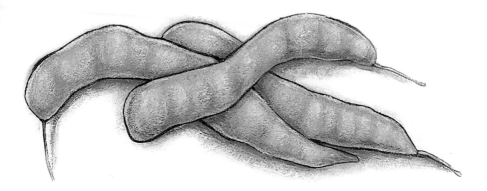

But when Charles sees
the best prize of all,

a frog, with big,
bulging eyes,

his pockets are just too full!

At night, Charles counts
out his treasures and
thinks about tomorrow.

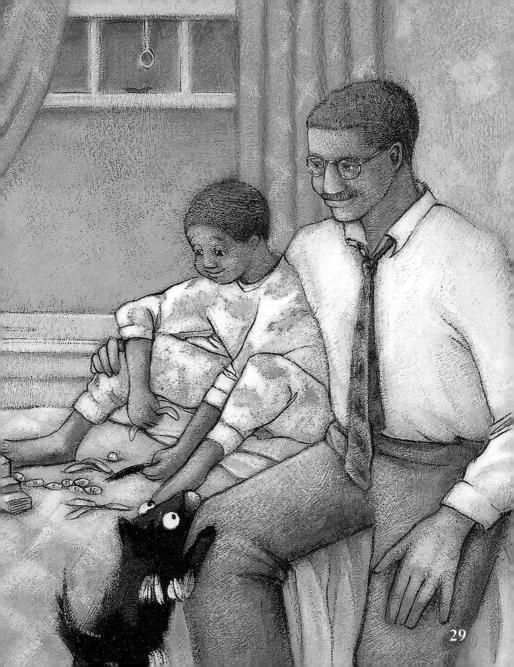